Who Stole Home Plate?

Who Stole
Home Plate?

A Southside Sluggers Baseball Mystery

Created by Glenn Lewis and Gail Tuchman
Written by Steven Otfinoski
Illustrated by Bert Dodson

SIMON & SCHUSTER BOOKS FOR YOUNG READERS
Published by Simon & Schuster
New York ♦ London ♦ Toronto ♦ Sydney ♦ Tokyo ♦ Singapore

SIMON & SCHUSTER BOOKS FOR YOUNG READERS
Simon & Schuster Building,
Rockefeller Center,
1230 Avenue of the Americas,
New York, New York 10020
Text copyright © 1992 by Glenn Lewis and Gail Tuchman.
Illustrations copyright © 1992 by Bert Dodson.
All rights reserved including the right of reproduction in whole or
in part in any form.
SIMON & SCHUSTER BOOKS FOR YOUNG READERS
is a trademark of Simon & Schuster.
Designed by Lucille Chomowicz.
The text of this book is set in Stempel Garamond.
The illustrations were done in black ink.
Also available in a LITTLE SIMON paperback edition. Series conceived and
text produced by Book Smart Inc. Manufactured in the United States of
America.
10 9 8 7 6 5 4 3 2 1   (pbk) 10 9 8 7 6 5 4 3 2 1
ISBN: 0-671-72928-4   ISBN: 0-671-72932-2 (pbk)

Contents

1 Intruder on the Field

Slowly and cautiously Rachel Langlin shifted her feet on first base, measuring in her mind the distance to second. She would need a big first step the moment the ball crossed home plate.

The pitcher on the mound was exchanging extra signals with the catcher. Rachel wasn't concerned. She felt confident she could beat any throw by any catcher.

The pitcher this time was her younger brother, Zach, and the catcher was her friend Andy West. And they were all on the same team—the Southside Sluggers. Yet even in a short Saturday morning practice game, Rachel's competitive spirit was as keen as ever. And so was her brother's.

Zach was now looking directly at Rachel on first base. *He's just trying to rattle me before going into his windup*, Rachel thought. But Rachel wasn't nicknamed "Stretch" by her teammates for nothing. She'd stretch a hit by going for an extra base at every opportunity. And she was always stretching her luck by trying to steal a base.

Zach twisted his tall, thin body through a windup and zipped the ball wide of home plate. Rachel exploded toward second as Andy jumped up to snag the ball in his mitt. It was a pitchout and Rachel was caught halfway between first and second. Andy hesitated for a moment and then whipped the ball to Marty Franklin at first when he saw Rachel running back. Rachel slid in under the tag by inches.

A whoop went up from the sidelines.

"Fast footwork!" cried Rachel's friend, center fielder Susan Stein.

"Another few feet and I could have made it to second!" replied Rachel.

"Another few inches and you would've been out!" cried Zach from the mound.

The next batter, Seth Bradigan, waited patiently at the plate for his first pitch. He swung his big bat, which he called "Thunderbolt," a few times to loosen up. Seth was probably the best all-around player on the Sluggers' team. And one of the most dependable power hitters in the Lotus Pines Youth Baseball League.

This time Rachel didn't waste a moment. On the first pitch to Seth she made her move. She tore off for second, head down, legs pumping. Seth swung and missed. Andy seized the ball and threw it to Luis Diaz at second base. Rachel was still a few feet from the base. Andy's throw had her beat easily. It looked like Rachel was going to be thrown out stealing for sure. But that's when something totally unexpected happened.

From out of nowhere, a furry ball of energy came charging across the base path. It was a small, tan shaggy dog. The dog's sudden appearance distracted Luis for a moment, just long enough for him to miss the ball. The ball grazed the top of his glove and went sailing into center field.

Since this was a practice game, and the Sluggers were split into two teams, there was no one in the outfield to retrieve the ball. Luis went tearing after it and Rachel went right on to third base. *Why steal one base, when you can take two?* she reasoned.

By the time Luis got the ball, Rachel had pulled up at third. The shaggy little dog ran around Rachel's legs a couple of times and then scampered off the field. It yelped and barked with excitement.

The whole team was laughing and pointing at the dog. But the team's coach was not amused by the spectacle.

"Keep that dog off the field!" Coach Terwilliger yelled. But no one even tried. It was too much fun to watch.

On the next pitch, Seth slashed a grounder to Luis at second base. At the same time, Rachel made her move to steal home. Andy took up his position in front of the plate for the throw from Luis.

Rachel was closing in fast with the little dog right

behind her. She dove, feet first, in a cloud of dust as Andy reached for the ball.

"Safe!" cried the coach.

The shaggy dog circled around Rachel, howling with delight.

"Where did that dog come from?" Coach Terwilliger demanded in his deep, gravelly voice.

"Beats me, Coach," admitted Rachel, getting to her feet. "But he sure showed up at the right moment."

"You can say that again," replied the coach. "If it wasn't for that silly pooch you would've been out for sure at second."

Rachel frowned, but said nothing. She thought the coach was being too tough on her. After all, she had made it from first to home plate just by stealing bases. That wasn't bad, even for a practice game.

The center of attention, however, was not Rachel but the intruding dog. The entire team had gathered around him at home plate. He was obviously enjoying all the attention and barking and wagging his tail at one and all.

"Look at him!" cried Seth. "He's acting like *he* scored the run!"

"Why, he's just a puppy!" said third-base player Michelle Brooks.

Coach Terwilliger was about to tell them to take their positions again, when the dog surprised everyone. Giving a big yawn, it began sniffing and circling the rubber plate. Finally, the dog just curled up on the plate as if it were a cozy rug.

"Can you beat that!" cried Zach. "That dog's taking a snooze on home plate!"

Shortstop Ernie Peters swished his cap at the dog. "Shoo! Shoo, doggie!" he yelled. "Go take your nap someplace else!"

The dog looked up at Ernie, cocked his head, and panted happily. Then he barked and gave another wag of his small furry tail.

Rachel laughed. "He thinks you want to play, Ernie," she said.

"He's right," said the coach. "We do want to play — play ball!"

The dog turned his big, brown eyes on Coach Terwilliger and whimpered.

"I think he likes you, Coach," grinned Andy.

The coach scratched his hair and stared at the dog. A faint smile crossed his face.

"He *is* kind of cute, isn't he?" Coach Terwilliger said. "Oh, well, I guess we've practiced enough for one day. But I want everyone back here at one o'clock tomorrow. You all need a lot more work if we're going to beat those Mudsharks in next Saturday's game."

The Mudsharks were the Southside Sluggers' arch-rivals in the Lotus Pines Youth Baseball League. Like the Sluggers, the Mudsharks had been at the bottom of the league last season. But now both teams were improving steadily. And each team saw the other as an obstacle on the road to a respectable season.

Rachel bent down and petted the strange dog on his shaggy head. "He sure is cute," she said. "I wonder who he belongs to?"

As if in answer to her question, Rachel felt a thin leather collar hidden under the dog's shaggy neck. She removed it.

A shiny medal dangled from the center of the collar. On it was stamped a picture of two crossed baseball bats and a baseball below them.

"It looks like some sort of insignia," said Seth.

"Maybe it's the insignia for a semipro baseball team," suggested Susan.

"Maybe," said Rachel, examining the medal more closely. "But the Lotus Pines Hawks' insignia doesn't look anything like this."

"Well, whoever owns this dog, we know he or she's definitely a baseball fan," said Andy.

"Which explains why the dog's hanging around Bloom Field," said Rachel. She strapped the collar back on the little dog's neck.

"I bet he ran away from home and got lost," said Zach.

"I doubt that," said the coach. "I bet he lives right here in the neighborhood. He'll go home when he's hungry."

The players agreed that the coach was probably right. Most of them headed out of Bloom Field Park and went their separate ways. But Rachel, Zach, Andy, and Seth lingered behind. The four friends continued to pet and talk to the dog. Rachel and the dog seemed to be growing particularly fond of each other.

"Come on, Rach," said her brother Zach. "Say good-bye to shaggy-face and let's hoof it home. I'm starved."

"You've got a *two*-track mind," replied his sister. "Baseball and food are all you care about—and not necessarily in that order."

But as Rachel got up and started to go, the dog looked up at her with hopeful eyes and barked.

"See you later, H.P.," she said, scratching the dog behind its ear. "You can come around here anytime."

"H.P.?" asked Zach.

"Short for Home Plate," explained Rachel.

Zach giggled. "That's not a bad name for a dog who's right at home there," he said. "Let's hope he's off our home plate by one o'clock tomorrow, though. I don't think the coach will like his practice being interrupted a second time."

2 A Home for Home Plate

If the Sluggers expected their new friend to be gone Sunday afternoon, they were to be pleasantly surprised. The shaggy little dog greeted them as they approached the ball field.

The only one who wasn't happy to see him was Coach Terwilliger. He was afraid the dog would disrupt their practice. But his fears soon melted away. The dog seemed to perk the kids up rather than get in their way.

Anticipating H.P.'s being there, Rachel had brought some leftovers from home in a plastic bag. She put them on the ground and the shaggy dog greedily ate every bite.

"Boy, he's got a bear-size appetite for such a little dog," marveled Andy.

"I have a feeling that he hasn't been fed since yesterday," said Rachel. "I don't think he's been home since we saw him last."

After eating, Home Plate—as Rachel and everybody else now called him—calmly lay down on a grassy spot near the first base line. From there, he watched the team practice with keen interest. The only times he got excited was when a batter hit the ball high into the air. Then he'd jump up and bark for joy.

During a break from practice, Rachel threw a rubber ball into the field and H.P. tore out after it. He grabbed the ball in his teeth and brought it back to her, time after time.

"He's a great retriever," said Andy.

"I can't understand why his owner isn't out looking for him," responded Rachel.

"Maybe he or she is and just hasn't looked here," said Seth.

"Well, if H.P. lives anywhere in the neighborhood, he'll probably get tired of watching us and go home before we leave the field today," added Zach. "Just like the coach said."

But when practice ended at four o'clock, H.P. was still sitting on the grass, wagging his furry tail. Rachel was beginning to worry. Just where did this dog come from? And how long would it be before somebody came by to take him home?

As the players prepared to leave, Mr. Clancy approached them from the stands. Mr. Clancy was an older man with thinning white hair who worked for the town. His job was to cut the grass and keep the baseball field in playing shape. He was also the official score-keeper for all the Youth League games. This seemed to be Mr. Clancy's favorite part of his job. He loved base-ball as much as any kid in the town of Lotus Pines.

Mr. Clancy was usually a friendly, outgoing man, but he didn't look very happy right now. He frowned at Home Plate and then turned to the group of Sluggers standing around the animal.

"Do any of you know who owns this dog?" he asked.

"We haven't a clue," said Michelle. "He just showed up at our practice on Saturday and he's been hanging around ever since."

"He's been hanging around, all right," sighed Mr. Clancy. "And that's the trouble."

"H.P.'s no trouble, Mr. Clancy," spoke up Rachel. "He just watches our practice."

"Well, he did more than watch at yesterday after-noon's game between the Sneakerama Bluesox and the Rocket Raiders," Mr. Clancy told them. "When one of the Raiders hit a bunt in the second inning, the dog went running after the ball and grabbed it before the pitcher could catch it."

Zach couldn't help laughing. "Andy is right. H.P.'s a great retriever," he joked.

"The coach for the Bluesox didn't find it so funny," continued Mr. Clancy. "The dog's interference gave the Raiders an easy double. Then in the next inning, the dog chased a grounder and tripped a Raider base run-ner who nearly ran right into him. The poor player was out at third. That got the Raiders' coach upset. By the end of the game the two coaches were ready to call the dog warden to take the dog away."

Rachel's eyes grew wild. "They can't do that!" she exclaimed. "Not to H.P.! He's got a collar!"

"They could, Rachel," said Mr. Clancy quietly. "The dog may have a collar, but there's no identification tag to prove who his owner is. He's a stray and he's fair game for the dog pound."

The six players standing around Home Plate looked at the dog happily gnawing on a marrowbone Rachel had brought.

"I talked them out of calling the dog warden," he explained. "Gosh, I've got two dogs of my own. I don't like to see any dog go to the pound. But the fact is, if he interferes in another game, something will have to be done about it. And as the person who's responsible for this ballpark, I'll have to be the one to do it."

Andy looked anxiously at Mr. Clancy. "You wouldn't call the dog warden to take H.P. away, would you, Mr. Clancy?" he asked.

Mr. Clancy patted H.P. affectionately on his woolly head. "Well, now," he said, "there'd be no need for that, if one of you were to adopt him and give him a home."

"That's it!" cried Rachel. "Someone can take H.P. home! Then he can come to the park anytime with us!"

"As long as he behaves himself," added Mr. Clancy.

"He does behave around us," said Seth. "It must have been the excitement of a game with all the people cheering and yelling in the stands that got him going."

"So who's going to adopt H.P.?" asked Rachel.

"Not us," spoke up Zach. "You know how Dad is about animals. His idea of the perfect pet is a goldfish."

"Right," agreed his sister. "Dad calls it 'low-maintenance animal care.'"

"Watch it, Sis," warned Zach. "Your vocabulary level is creeping up again." Rachel's fondness for fancy words was a constant frustration for her more down-to-earth brother.

"I'm sure one of you other guys can give H.P. a good home," Rachel said.

Robin Hayes, the Sluggers' relief pitcher, smiled and shook her head. "I'd love to adopt him," she admitted. "But my sister has a cat who's really dog shy. If I brought H.P. home, I'd have one big fight on my hands."

"You mean between the cat and the dog?" asked Andy.

"No," grinned Robin, "between me and my sister."

Rachel turned to the Sluggers' third-base player. "How about you, Michelle?"

"Sorry," replied Michelle. "One of the rules for all residents in the apartment complex we live in is—"

"I know, no pets!" Zach finished. "Seth, how about you?"

"You guys all know I already have a dog," replied the left fielder.

"We know," said Rachel, "but wouldn't King like a buddy—a friend to keep him company?"

"You don't know King very well," replied Seth. "He likes being top dog at our house. He might enjoy having H.P. for a friend but not for a housemate.

Besides, it was hard enough to get my dad to let me have one dog. He'd never go for another one."

"We can't even have *one* dog at our house," spoke up Andy. "My mom's allergic to them."

"You're kidding!" exclaimed Robin.

"It's the truth," said Andy. "She gets anywhere near a dog and she breaks out in hives."

"Well, *somebody's* got to take H.P.," said Rachel. "We can't just let him be carted off to the dog pound."

"It's not so bad," said Mr. Clancy. "I mean, lots of people adopt dogs from the pound. H.P.'s such a cute dog, someone is sure to want him."

"Maybe," said Michelle. "But if someone doesn't take him home in thirty days, the people at the pound will put him to sleep."

"That does it," said Rachel firmly. "Zach, H.P.'s coming home with us."

"Come on, Sis," said Zach. "You know Dad will never go for that."

"It'll only be temporary," reasoned Rachel. "We'll put up signs around town. Maybe his owner will see one and come to claim him."

"What do you think, H.P.?" she asked, bending down to the shaggy dog. "Do you want to come home with Zach and me?"

"Rrrrrufff!" replied the dog. Then he started to lick Rachel's face with his scratchy pink tongue.

The others laughed, even Mr. Clancy.

"He'd better not do that to Dad," said Zach, "or we'll *all* be in the doghouse tonight!"

3 A New Mascot

"Well, kids, how did your practice go?" asked Mr. Langlin.

"Fine, Dad," said Zach, taking a chair at the dinner table.

Mr. Langlin was a tall, thin man with hair as red as his daughter's. He wasn't interested in the Sluggers just because Zach and Rachel played on the team. He was the owner of the Southside Ice Cream Shop, located in the Southside section of Lotus Pines. He was also the team's sole sponsor. This explained the Sluggers' odd green-and-orange uniforms. They matched two of Mr. Langlin's most famous ice-cream flavors, which he invented himself—Pickleberry Sundae and Orang-u-tang Chip.

"Glad to hear it was a good practice," said Mr. Langlin. "Is the coach working with you on your base stealing, Rachel?"

Rachel tucked in her napkin and rolled her eyes. "I stole three bases and scored a run at practice yesterday," she said. "I don't think I need much help from the coach, Dad. But he is working with me."

"That's wonderful, Rachel," said Aunt Pearl.

Aunt Pearl was Mrs. Langlin's sister. She lived on the other side of town. But she joined the family for dinner at least once a week.

"It's not all that wonderful," argued Zach. "She wouldn't have made it to second if it hadn't been for H.P."

Rachel gave her brother a cross look and kicked him under the table.

"Who's H.P.?" asked Mr. Langlin.

Just then Mrs. Langlin entered from the kitchen with a covered dish.

"Uh, what's for dinner, Mom?" asked Rachel, anxious to change the subject.

"Your father's favorite—meat loaf," replied Mrs. Langlin. "Zach, will you go get the vegetables, please?"

"Sure, Mom," said Zach.

"Who's H.P.?" Mr. Langlin asked for the second time.

"Oh, nobody," said Rachel. Rachel was telling the truth. Home Plate wasn't a person, just a dog. She wanted to prepare her father slowly for the dog and Zach had practically blown that plan to bits.

Rachel waited until halfway through the meal before she raised the crucial question.

"Wouldn't it be nice if we had a pet?" she said off-handedly to no one in particular.

"We already do," said her father as he buttered a piece of Aunt Pearl's homemade bread.

"A goldfish isn't a *real* pet, Dad," Rachel argued. "It just sits there all day in its bowl. You can't play with it or take it for a walk."

"Exactly," said Mr. Langlin. "That's why fish make such great pets. No fuss, no bother. Low-maintenance animal care, I call it."

Zach grinned at his sister across the table, remembering her words earlier that afternoon.

"That's true," said Rachel. "But wouldn't it be nice to have a pet we could have some *real* fun with?"

"You mean, like a cat?" asked Aunt Pearl.

"That's right, a cat . . . or a dog," said Rachel slowly.

Mr. Langlin looked at his daughter and lowered his fork from his mouth. "We've been over this before, Rachel," he said. "You and Zach are out practicing and playing ball all summer. Who would get stuck taking care of your pet? Me and your mother, that's who."

"No," protested Rachel. "I promise I'd walk it and feed it and clean up after it. Honest, Dad."

"But you wouldn't have to walk a *cat*, dear," said Mrs. Langlin.

"I think Rachel and Zach are old enough to have a pet of their own," spoke up Aunt Pearl. "As long as they're willing to take care of it."

Mr. Langlin looked very thoughtful. "It's true a cat can pretty much take care of itself," he said. "They're very independent, not like dogs."

Zach looked at his sister and shook his head as if to say, *You got yourself into this one. Now let's see how you're going to get out of it.*

"Actually, Dad, what I was thinking of was—" Rachel began.

She was suddenly interrupted by a strange noise at the back door.

"What was that?" asked Mr. Langlin.

Rachel felt a sinking feeling in her stomach. "I'm sure it was nothing," she said.

"There it is again," said Mr. Langlin, getting to his feet. He quickly crossed to the back door and opened it. There was H.P., tongue lolling and tail wagging, staring up at Mr. Langlin.

"What's this dog doing in our backyard?" Mr. Langlin asked.

"Rrrufffff!" barked H.P.

"I thought you tied him to the tree," Rachel said accusingly to her brother.

"I did," said Zach. "He must've gotten loose."

"I'm waiting for an answer to my question," said Mr. Langlin.

Rachel took a deep breath. "Dad," she said, "meet H.P.—the newest member of the Southside Sluggers."

Mr. Langlin stared at the dog, his eyes widening. "You mean this dog helped you steal those bases?" he asked.

"He sure did," said Zach quickly. "H.P. loves base-

ball, Pop. He's been at Bloom Field for both yesterday's and today's practice."

"He's a baseball dog, huh?" said Mr. Langlin.

Rachel could've kissed her brother right then. If there was one way to get to their father's heart it was to bring up his favorite sport.

"He really is cute, Fred," said Aunt Pearl.

"And he's just a puppy," said Mrs. Langlin.

"He is," admitted Mr. Langlin. "And puppies require a lot more care than grown dogs do."

"I'll take care of him," vowed Rachel. "You won't have to worry about a thing."

"I'll help too," said Zach.

"As long as you two take care of him, it's okay with me if he stays," said Mrs. Langlin.

"Besides," added Rachel, "it'll probably only be temporary. We're going to put up signs to see if we can find his owner."

"I don't know . . . ," said Mr. Langlin, still undecided.

"Dad," said Rachel boldly. "H.P. is going to be our team mascot."

A new look came into her father's green eyes.

"Mascot, huh?" Mr. Langlin said. "That's not a bad idea. No other team in the league has a mascot. It could be a great attraction, increase game attendance, and give the Sluggers a big morale boost. I could talk to the editor of the *Lotus Times*. Why, I bet we could even get the dog's picture in the paper—wearing the team colors, of course. What does H.P. stand for?"

"Home Plate," said Rachel. "I thought it up."

Mr. Langlin laughed. "That's great! All right. H.P. can move in—for a trial period. If he behaves himself and you two take full responsibility for him, he can stay until we find his owner."

"Gee, thanks!" cried Rachel, hugging her father and then her mother.

"Ruff! Ruff!" barked H.P., who seemed to understand he had found a new home—at least for now.

Aunt Pearl scooped H.P. up in her arms and Mrs. Langlin patted his fur.

"Welcome to your new home!" said Mrs. Langlin.

Zach drew his sister aside.

"Team mascot?" he said.

"Sure, why not?" replied Rachel.

"Well, let's hope Coach Terwilliger thinks it's as great an idea as Dad does," Zach said.

4 One Base Too Many

Rachel's mascot idea may have been a desperate move to get her father to let her keep Home Plate. However, it appealed to all the Sluggers Rachel and Zach spoke to as much as it did to Mr. Langlin. The entire team was enthusiastic about having a team mascot, even Coach Terwilliger.

"But the coach said H.P. has to be on a leash when we bring him out before a game," Zach told Rachel. "He doesn't want our mascot running wild on the field. He said it wouldn't look good."

Rachel readily agreed with what the coach had said. She remembered how the dog had disrupted the Raiders–Bluesox game and the problems he had caused for Mr. Clancy.

Right after school on Monday, Rachel, Zach, Seth,

and Andy put up Lost Dog signs in several supermarkets and stores. They included the Langlins' address and phone number on the signs. None of them really wanted H.P. to be claimed, though.

Then Mr. Langlin took Zach and Rachel down to the local pet store. They picked out a nice leather leash for H.P. It was long enough to allow H.P. as much freedom as possible. Rachel got him a squeaky rubber toy and Zach picked out a rubber ball.

Early Saturday morning, the day of the game against the Mudsharks, Aunt Pearl arrived. Mrs. Langlin had suggested that she come over and help get H.P. cleaned up for his debut. Rachel, Zach, Mrs. Langlin, and Aunt Pearl gave him a bubble bath in the backyard. While they bathed H.P., Aunt Pearl told the children how he reminded her of a little dog she had many years before.

There wasn't time to get H.P. dressed in the team colors, as Mr. Langlin had wanted. Aunt Pearl had begun knitting a special sweater for him, but it wasn't finished yet. Instead, she tried a Sluggers' cap on the dog's head after they dried him off. H.P. didn't seem to mind the cap. But as soon as he moved, it flopped off his woolly head.

Aunt Pearl ran a string through the cap so it could be tied securely onto the dog's head.

"Now he looks like a real baseball dog!" Mrs. Langlin exclaimed.

An hour later, the Mudsharks and the fans in the stands

looked on with surprise. Rachel came strolling onto Bloom Field with Home Plate before the game. The dog walked proudly ahead of her, wearing the baseball cap.

Once they got over their surprise, a few of the Mudsharks, led by their right fielder, Billy Butler, began to laugh and hoot.

"What is this?" asked Billy. "A ball game or a three-ring circus?"

H.P. barked at the Mudsharks, but Rachel chose to ignore the remark.

"This is our new mascot," replied Rachel coolly. "Mudsharks, meet H.P.—short for 'Home Plate.'"

"You mean short for 'Hairy Pooch,' don't you?" laughed Sarah Fine, the Mudsharks' second base player.

But the crowd in the stands found H.P. a charming addition to the game. They seemed to enjoy watching the dog as much as they did the Sluggers and the Mudsharks. Every time a Slugger got a hit, H.P. would bark wildly and run back and forth on his patch of grass near the bench. Even the Mudsharks had to agree that this was one dog who loved baseball.

As for the Sluggers, H.P.'s presence did seem to boost their morale, just as Mr. Langlin had predicted. Their batting was better than usual and their fielding was in top form.

Zach "The Tongue" Langlin's pitching was pretty sharp against the Mudsharks too. He pitched two scoreless innings and had a lot of hop on his fastball.

Then the coach brought Robin Hayes into the game.

He figured her tricky off-speed pitches would keep the Mudsharks off balance. Robin's early relief appearance would also free up Zach for four innings of pitching in the Mudshark makeup game on Tuesday.

Seth "Clear Out" Bradigan helped to tighten up the outfield. He made one fantastic catch after another. Earlier in the season when he first joined the team, Seth had hogged the outfield and forced other players to "clear out." But now Seth had learned how to share the turf and back up the players around him.

One team member, however, had not yet lived down her nickname—Rachel "Stretch" Langlin. She still stretched each play to its limit and beyond—both as a fielder and as a base runner.

Once again Rachel reached too far—this time in the third inning. Mudshark heavy hitter Chip Hoover slammed a hot grounder to shortstop Ernie "Hippity Hop" Peters. Ernie, as usual, hopped up and down in nervous anticipation of the speeding ball and lost his timing. He fumbled the catch and Chip reached first safely.

The next batter was the Mudsharks' Big Joe Jones. Joe was big in both size and batting power. After a careless strike and two balls, Joe clobbered the ball deep to right field.

Running back, Rachel stretched her glove upward and caught the speeding ball in her webbing. Chip, who had started to run toward second, stopped short and hustled back toward first.

Rachel should have been happy with her catch and the one out. But she wasn't. Rachel believed she could catch Chip off base with a rushed throw to Marty Franklin at first. She needed a perfectly on-target peg from deep in the outfield.

Rachel quickly reared back and heaved the ball toward first. Her hurried throw sailed high and wide of the base. Marty made a huge leap to catch it, but didn't get close.

Out of danger from being tagged at first, Chip decided to run for second. Andy retrieved the ball at home, but wasn't able to fling it fast enough to second baseman Luis Diaz.

"Safe at second!" cried out the umpire.

Rachel kicked at the dirt in disgust. She had blown it but good.

"Go on," she said to center fielder Susan Stein. "Tell me I blew it!"

Susan just smiled. She knew Rachel was a solid all-round player. If anything, Rachel tended to be harder on herself than anybody else could be. So why point out an obvious mistake?

"It's okay, Rach," she said calmly. "Just don't feel you have to stretch every play. You caught the ball and that was enough."

"It's no use," sighed Rachel. "I just can't seem to help myself."

Rachel decided to play more cautiously for the rest of the game. But the damage had already been done. Phil Woods, the next Mudsharks batter, hit a solid double to left field that even the usually reliable Seth couldn't touch. The hit brought Chip Hoover home and put the Mudsharks ahead, 1-0.

It was the Sluggers' turn at bat. Robin Hayes, batting ninth for Zach, struck out. This brought up Rachel—the Sluggers' lead-off batter. She was determined to make up for her earlier error by getting a big hit.

Mudsharks pitcher Ken Allan got a quick strike on Rachel with his change-up. But, when he threw the same pitch again, Rachel was ready for it.

She sent the ball flying over Ken's head into shallow center field. The clean single put Rachel on first with only one out.

Susan was a dependable hitter with almost a .300 batting average. She stepped up to the plate with confidence. The pitcher looked carefully around the bases before his windup, pausing at first base. He eyed Rachel closely.

He's warning me not to try to steal a base, Rachel thought. *If he thinks he's going to scare me that easily, he's dead wrong.* She had no intention of forfeiting her reputation as the league's busiest base stealer.

Susan now had no balls and one strike against her. With one out already, Rachel feared she might never get off first. As the pitch crossed the plate, Rachel tore off for second.

Susan swung and missed. The catcher whipped the ball straight to second. Rachel had to stop between the two bases and turn back. She sprinted toward first, but the ball beat her easily.

"Out!" cried the umpire.

Rachel punched the air in frustration. She had

nobody to blame but herself and she knew it. Coach Terwilliger couldn't have agreed with her more.

"I don't want you to steal another base this game," he told her when she returned to the bench. "It's not worth the risk."

"I thought it was," protested Rachel weakly. "I thought I had nothing to lose."

"You had plenty to lose and you lost it," replied the coach sternly. "We had only one out and a runner on base. You made it two outs with nobody on base. If you'd waited, Seth or Susan might have brought you home with a hit."

Coach Terwilliger saw Rachel's downcast face and smiled.

"Look, everybody makes mistakes, Rachel," he continued. "Just be more cautious next time."

"Don't be so nice, Coach," Rachel replied. "My steal attempt may have cost us the game."

Susan hit a sharp double to left field and Seth followed with a solid triple off the center-field fence. Another single brought Seth home. This made the score Sluggers 2, Mudsharks 1. If Rachel hadn't tried to steal, the Sluggers might have had three runs that inning.

The Sluggers produced two more runs in the second half of the game. The Mudsharks chalked up four more runs—thanks to a grand-slam homer by Big Joe Jones. At the end of the game, the score was Mudsharks 5, Sluggers 4. The run Rachel threw away would have put the game into extra innings.

Big Joe, Chip Hoover, and Billy Butler ran around the field with their arms in the air. They called the Sluggers silly names—"Whiffers," "Chokers," and "Losers." And they offered "Stretch" Langlin a map to find second base.

Even the sight of Home Plate wagging his tail and barking happily didn't lift Rachel's spirits much. She knew she had let down her team and her coach.

"Next time you want to steal something, try something easier, like an elephant," cracked Zach as they walked home after the game.

Rachel knew her brother was just trying to cheer her up. "I'm not in the mood for your witticisms," she said, shaking her red braids. "Amusing though they may be."

"Witti—what?" sputtered Zach. He knew his sister was just trying to get his goat. And she had succeeded.

"Witticism, jest, *bon mot*," shot back his sister impatiently.

Zach stopped walking and drew himself up to his full five feet and seven inches. "Okay! That does it!" he exclaimed. "I can deal with the fancy words, but when you start talking in Latin, you've gone too far!"

Rachel laughed, in spite of her bad mood. "It's French, not Latin," she explained. "*Bon mot* is French for a clever remark!"

Zach was about to come back with another snappy witticism when their conversation was suddenly interrupted. A yellow cat with white stripes appeared on the sidewalk in front of them. At first sight of the cat,

Home Plate howled loudly and lunged forward. The sudden move caught Rachel off guard and she lost her grip on H.P.'s leash. The cat meowed and went flying down the block, with Home Plate in hot pursuit.

"Oh, great!" cried Zach. "Just what we need. That's Mr. Leopold's cat!"

"Come on," replied his sister. "We've got to catch H.P. before he catches the cat."

Mr. Leopold was the Langlins' next-door neighbor. He had two main interests outside his family and job — his rose garden and his cat, Maisy. He was fiercely protective of both. Rachel recalled how once she had accidentally stepped in one of his rose beds while chasing after a stray ball. Mr. Leopold had gotten so upset he had threatened to phone the police.

The cat scurried into the Leopolds' driveway with H.P. yelping right behind it. By the time Rachel and Zach arrived at the same spot, Maisy was safely sheltered in Mr. Leopold's short, chubby arms. Home Plate was barking at his feet.

"Don't you lay a paw on my poor Maisy, you mangy mutt!" yelled Mr. Leopold.

"He's not a mutt," shot back Rachel — then instantly reconsidered what she had said. "Well, maybe he is a mutt. But he's our mutt. And he's not at all mangy."

Mr. Leopold stared at the two Langlin children with disbelief. "You mean to say that's *your* dog?" he asked.

"That's right," spoke up Zach bravely. "We just got him last Sunday."

"I thought your parents had better sense than to let

you have a dog," grumbled their neighbor. He said the word *dog* as if it were some kind of annoying insect.

"We're sorry that Home Plate chased your cat, Mr. Leopold," said Rachel. "But I'm sure he was just playing. After all, he is a puppy."

"His age has nothing to do with it," replied the cat lover. "No dog can be trusted around a cat. You just keep that dog of yours away from my Maisy or he'll be sorry."

Zach sighed. "Don't worry, we will," he said.

Rachel picked up H.P. Then the three of them quickly headed for their own yard.

"You remember what I said!" Mr. Leopold called after them.

"Guess we'd better keep a good grip on H.P.'s leash when we take him out," said Zach, as they walked into their house. "Or we might lose our *ewnay ascotmay*."

Rachel stared at her brother, her blue eyes opened wide.

"What's that?" she asked.

"Pig Latin for 'new mascot,'" Zach explained with a grin. "You're not the only one who can talk in a foreign language, you know."

Just then the shrill ring of the telephone interrupted their conversation. Rachel raced into the kitchen to answer it.

The answering machine was on and the taped announcement was rolling. The announcement ended and Coach Terwilliger's familiar gravelly voice was heard—but the tape made his voice sound a bit off-speed.

"Rachel, this is the coach. . . ."

Rachel picked up the telephone and shut off the machine.

"Is that you, Coach?" she said. "What's up?"

"Oh, hi," replied the coach. "I'd like to see you Monday afternoon for a special little practice session, if you can make it. I want to work with you on your baserunning before our makeup game against the Mudsharks on Tuesday."

"I guess I can make it," said Rachel slowly. "But do you really think I need the practice? I'm the fastest runner on the team, Coach."

"The fastest, maybe, but not the most thoughtful," replied Coach Terwilliger. "Speed alone doesn't make a really good base stealer, Rachel. You need to sharpen up your judgment and control a bit."

"Okay, Coach," said Rachel, embarrassed about the special instruction session, "I'll see you on the field on Monday."

"Tell Zach to be there too," added the coach. "We'll need a pitcher to just toss a few in there. I'll call a few other players as well."

Rachel thanked the coach for calling and hung up. Zach was standing behind her in the kitchen.

"The coach is calling an extra practice?" he asked her.

"For me, personally," Rachel told him. "I guess I can use it, too. But it makes me feel so silly getting extra instruction."

"It's a compliment," said Zach. "The coach knows

that your baserunning could be a big help to the team if you used it right."

"I guess so," said Rachel, feeling a little better. "I don't know why Dad bothers to turn on the answering machine anymore," she added, changing the subject. "The message tape is so worn out, you can barely understand a word on it. He needs to replace the tape."

To demonstrate her point, Rachel rewound the tape and played the coach's brief message. It came out so garbled that Zach couldn't even make it out.

"The coach sounds even more gravel-voiced than he does in real life!" laughed Zach.

"I'll be sure to tell him you said that," grinned Rachel.

"Don't you dare," kidded Zach. "He'll have me running bases all afternoon alongside you!"

Suddenly, the phone rang again. Rachel answered it. It was Seth.

"How's our favorite mascot?" he asked.

"Fine," said Rachel.

"Well, you take good care of him," Seth said. "He's worth his weight in baseballs."

"What do you mean?" Rachel asked.

"I mean, thanks to H.P., we're the hottest team in town," replied Seth.

"Even after losing today to the Mudsharks?" asked Rachel.

"That's just one game," said Seth. "We'll spring back when we play them again on Tuesday. The important thing is that news about H.P. has spread all over town. He's the biggest thing to hit the Lotus Pines Youth Baseball League since they put in the new grandstands at Bloom Field."

Rachel's face was a blank. "Are you serious?" she said.

"Every team wants a mascot now," explained Seth. "I've heard the Rocket Raiders and the Sneakerama Bluesox are both looking for an animal to represent them on the field."

"How about the Mudsharks?" asked Rachel.

"You know the Mudsharks," said Seth. "They're too busy making fun of our mascot to admit it's a good idea."

"Well, no matter what mascot those other teams get, none of them will top H.P.," Rachel said. "He was the first and he's the best. And maybe we'll stay lucky and no one will come to claim him."

"I sure hope not," said Seth before he hung up.

Rachel told her brother about Seth's news.

"If the Mudsharks get a mascot," Zach said, "it should be a weasel or, better yet, a worm. That would be the perfect symbol for those belly crawlers."

Soon after, Mr. Langlin arrived home.

Rachel told her father about the problem with the message tape. He decided to go downtown and get a new tape for the answering machine. Rachel and Zach said they'd go with him.

Rachel thought about bringing H.P. along, but her father and Zach said the dog would be too much trouble inside the store. Rachel agreed and tied him on a long rope to an old oak tree in the backyard. Then she filled his water and food bowls and left them near him.

Mrs. Langlin was out but would be home shortly. Rachel knew she'd watch out for H.P. until they got back.

When Rachel arrived back home, she ran into the backyard to see how H.P. was. The rope was still there, tied securely to the tree. But H.P. was not.

5 Dognapped!

"Where's H.P.?" Zach asked, coming up behind Rachel.

"I don't know," she said. "Maybe Mom took him inside the house or for a walk."

But when they went into the house, they found their mother in the kitchen cooking. She looked surprised by their questions.

"I thought H.P. was with you," she said.

"You mean you didn't see him in the backyard?" asked Rachel.

"No, when I got back ten minutes ago, he wasn't there," replied Mrs. Langlin.

"Now let's not get too worried," said Mr. Langlin. "The dog probably got loose from the rope and is running around the neighborhood. We'll find him."

But a quick search of the immediate neighborhood turned up no sign of Home Plate.

"He's got to be around here somewhere," said Mr. Langlin. "How far can a small dog get on his own?"

"But H.P. wouldn't run away, Dad," insisted Rachel. "He liked it here. He liked us."

"That may be true," agreed her father, "but he ran away from home before, didn't he? I mean, how did he end up in Bloom Field in the first place?"

Zach snapped his fingers. "Bloom Field!" he exclaimed. "If H.P ran away, that's the most likely place he would go!"

"You're right," agreed Rachel. "When we left to go downtown, he might have thought we were going to another ball game. He wanted to go too. He got loose and went to the ball field looking for us!"

"It's worth a look," said Mr. Langlin. "Hop in the car. I'll drive you over there."

"That's okay, Dad," said Rachel. "Zach and I can ride our bikes. It's better if you drive around the neighborhood to look for H.P."

"I'll come with you," said Mrs. Langlin to her husband. "Rachel's right. We've got to spread our forces out as much as possible."

Bloom Field was about a mile from the Langlins' home and it took Rachel and Zach less than ten minutes to pedal their bikes there. They found Andy and Seth batting a ball around on the diamond. The two friends were surprised to see Zach and Rachel.

"Have you seen H.P.?" asked Rachel breathlessly.

"No," replied Seth. "Isn't he with you?"

Rachel briefly explained what had happened.

"That's terrible!" exclaimed Andy. "We've got to find him right away. We can't play our game against the Mudsharks on Tuesday without our good-luck mascot."

Seth had a bright idea. "We'll put out an all-team alert," he said. "We'll have Sluggers searching every corner of Lotus Pines for H.P. We'll find him in no time."

Rachel, looking unconvinced, sat down on the bench. "*If* he can be found at all," she said glumly.

"What do you mean, Sis?" asked Zach. Suddenly a dark look came over Zach's long, pale face. "You don't think he was run over by a car or something like that, do you?"

"No," replied Rachel. "H.P. is too smart a dog to get hit by a car. Look at how long he survived on his own in Bloom Field. What I mean is, maybe he didn't run away at all. Maybe somebody came into our back-yard and *took* him."

"You mean, dognapped him?" asked Seth.

"Exactly," said Rachel.

"Who'd want to steal Home Plate?" asked Andy.

"Our neighbor Mr. Leopold, for one," said Rachel. "He was hopping mad today when H.P. chased his old cat. He told us H.P. would be sorry if he did it again."

"But that was just today," reasoned Andy. "H.P. couldn't have chased his cat again, could he?"

Zach sighed and shook his head. "H.P. *did* chase the

cat again," he admitted. "Before, when you were talking on the phone, Sis. H.P. saw Maisy crossing the sidewalk in front of our house and took off after her. I got him back in the house, but he gave that cat a good fright."

Rachel looked excited. "Did Mr. Leopold see you and H.P.?" she asked.

"He might've," said Zach.

"Anyway, that definitely gives him a reason for taking H.P.," said Rachel. "Now, are there any other suspects with a motive—you know, a reason—for stealing our mascot?"

"The Mudsharks!" cried Andy. "They were green with envy at the game today. When they saw how much everyone liked H.P., they could've just burst."

"That's right," chimed in Zach. "Stealing our mascot before our next game with them is just the kind of mean thing the Mudsharks would do."

"Maybe we should pay a visit to a few of the Mudsharks and see what they know," suggested Seth.

Rachel glanced up at the sky. "It's a little late," she said. "Zach and I have to get home for dinner. Besides, our parents may have found H.P. or maybe he's come home by himself. If not, we'll call both of you tomorrow and plan our strategy."

"Call us either way," said Andy. "We want to know what's happening—bad or good."

Rachel promised she'd call and they all started out of the park on their bikes. They were only a few blocks away when they saw a familiar figure on a bike. On the

opposite side of the street, Billy Butler was pedaling like mad.

Zach called out to him, but the traffic noises drowned him out. It was doubtful Billy would have heard him anyway. He was concentrating totally on pedaling. In his bike basket was a large crumpled grocery bag. Out of it protruded several large marrowbones.

"I wonder where he's going," said Seth.

"Wherever it is, he's sure in an awful hurry," observed Zach.

Rachel's eyes narrowed. "Does Billy Butler have a dog?" she asked.

"Not that I know of," replied Andy.

"Then what does he want with all those bones?" wondered Rachel aloud.

A bright gleam came into Zach's blue eyes. "You don't think that maybe he—"

"I don't know, but he is a Mudshark, isn't he?" asked Rachel. "Come on. Let's follow him."

"What about your dinner?" asked Andy.

"Mom and Dad will understand if we're a little late," said Rachel. "Especially if we catch some dognappers!"

Zach agreed and the four friends started to pedal after Billy Butler as he turned his bike down a side street.

6 Big Secret at Daisy Park

Down one side street after another Billy Butler rode with the four Sluggers a safe distance behind him. They wisely decided if they followed him too closely he might become suspicious.

After ten minutes of this, Seth began to wonder if they weren't on a wild goose chase. "Look, guys," he said, "it's getting late. Maybe Billy's just going home."

Zach shook his head. "We passed Billy's street three blocks ago. He's taking those bones somewhere else."

Just then they saw Billy turn into a tree-lined street. A sign on a white post on the corner read: DAISY PARK.

"Daisy Park!" exclaimed Rachel. "This is really getting interesting!"

Daisy Park was one of Lotus Pines's less-used public

parks. Like Bloom Field, it had a baseball field. But the Lotus Pines Youth Baseball League played there only if Bloom Field was unavailable.

Daisy Park was a more natural park than Bloom Field Park. It had a woods, a pond, and an abundance of wildflowers and bushes of every description. Because of its rugged appearance, the park attracted fewer picnickers and families. It was the perfect place to hide a dog.

"What would Billy Butler be doing at Daisy Park this late in the day with a bag of bones?" asked Andy.

"You can bet he's not going to feed the squirrels with them," said Seth.

"Or going on a picnic," joked Zach. "Unless he's gone on a new diet."

"Fat chance," snapped Rachel. "Billy likes eating better than he likes baseball. I've got a feeling that he's about to lead us to Home Plate."

"You really think the Mudsharks stole H.P. out of your yard?" asked Andy.

"Why not?" said Zach. "We've already figured out that they have a good motive. And what better place to hide H.P. than in Daisy Park?"

"That's right," agreed Seth. "They couldn't take him to one of their homes. Their parents would start asking too many questions. They have to hide him somewhere no one would see him. Or think to look for him."

Rachel pointed up the road to where Billy and his bike were fading into the lengthening shadows. "Let's save the talk for later," she said. "We don't want to lose Billy. Daisy Park is big and in this light we might not find him again."

The others agreed and raced up the road on their bikes. Billy slowed down, and so did they. He seemed relaxed now, as if he was about to reach his final destination.

Billy pulled his bike off the road just before the park's small parking lot. Then he started pedaling up a sloping grassy hillside.

"The woods are on the other side of that hill," cautioned Seth. "If they took H.P., that would be the place where they'd keep him. We'd better leave our bikes here and creep up on foot."

"This is getting exciting," said Andy, dropping his bike on the grass. "I feel like a sheriff sneaking up on some cow rustlers."

"You mean dog rustlers," said Zach.

Seth and Andy laughed. Rachel frowned at them. "From here on we'd better not talk above a whisper," said Rachel. "We want to find out exactly what the Mudsharks are up to. If they discover us before we want them to, it might just ruin everything."

Zach moved his thumb and forefinger across his mouth, as if he were zipping it shut. Then he led the way up the grassy slope. They reached the top and looked down. The setting sun cast long, gloomy shadows across every tree and tall bush below.

At the edge of the woods, Billy Butler was greeted by two shadowy figures. The crouching foursome were just near enough to hear their conversation.

"Well, it's about time," said an impatient voice that the Sluggers recognized as belonging to Mudshark Chip Hoover.

"What took you so long?" asked the third person.

"I'm sorry I'm late. I had to eat dinner with my folks," explained Billy weakly.

"Okay," said the third person, who Rachel now recognized as Sarah Fine. "What did you bring for him?"

"Marrowbones," replied Billy, holding up the paper bag. "I got them from the butcher."

"Good," said Chip, inspecting the bag's contents. "They'll do for now. Tomorrow we'll go out and buy some real dog food for him. He can't live on bones, you know."

Billy was disappointed that his efforts weren't better appreciated. "Dog food?" he asked. "How much is that going to cost?"

"Don't worry," said Chip. "We'll take it out of the team fund."

"Come on," said Sarah. "Let's give him the bones."

The four friends on the hilltop looked at each other. Zach was about to say something, when Rachel held a finger to her lips. Then, silently, they crept down the hill and followed the three Mudsharks into the wooded area.

They watched the Mudsharks enter a small clearing surrounded by thick bushes. The Mudsharks had completed the camouflage themselves, placing broken tree branches and other debris on top of the bushes. They had gone to a lot of trouble to create a secret hiding place.

The Sluggers stopped before the opening in the bushes where the Mudsharks had gone. Rachel crouched down and peered through the thick greenery.

"Can you see anything?" whispered Andy.

"Barely," she replied softly. "The bushes are thick and it's pretty dark. They're standing around a tall tree in the center of the clearing and it looks like an animal's tied to the tree."

Just then a loud barking broke the still air.

"It's H.P.!" cried Zach.

"Quiet!" whispered Seth hoarsely. "They'll hear us!"

Seth, Zach, and Andy drew closer to the bushes and tried to peer through them into the clearing. They couldn't see any more than Rachel, but they could clearly hear every word spoken by the three Mudsharks.

"Look at him go for those bones!" exclaimed Chip.

"How long are we going to keep him here?" asked Billy, sounding a little worried.

"Till Tuesday morning," said Chip. "Then we'll move him to Bloom Field for the game."

"Did you hear that?" Zach whispered to his friends. "They're going to take *our* mascot to the game. Talk about nerve!"

Suddenly the conversation on the other side of the bushes stopped.

"Did you hear something?" Sarah Fine asked her two friends.

"Hear what?" said Billy.

"I could have sworn I just heard someone talking in the bushes," she replied.

The Sluggers held their breaths and waited.

"I don't hear anything," said Chip. "It must've been the crickets you heard."

Sarah listened for a minute. Everything was silent except for the *trrr* sound of the cricket's song.

"Guess you're right," she said. "We'd better be going. It's getting late."

"So we're just going to leave him here?" asked Billy.

"He'll be all right," said Chip. "He's used to sleeping outside. I'll come by tomorrow and take him for a long walk around the park."

"Good idea," said Sarah. "He'll need his exercise. We want him to be in top shape for the game. Just think of the expression on those Sluggers' faces when they see *our* mascot."

Zach started to get up when he heard these words, but Andy and Seth stopped him.

"Can you believe it!" Zach said in a low voice. "They're going to make H.P. *their* mascot! What nerve!"

Rachel leaned over and whispered in her brother's ear. "I know! But let's not do anything yet," she said. "Once they're gone we can untie H.P. and take him home. Then they'll be the ones who'll be surprised, right?"

Zach smiled and nodded. He had to agree that it was a better idea than confronting the Mudsharks in the clearing. By stealing back their dog they would be giving the Mudsharks a taste of their own medicine.

The Sluggers moved back from the opening in the bushes as Billy, Chip, and Sarah were about to leave the clearing.

"Ouch!" Andy cried, as the sharp thorns from a brier bush scratched his left forearm.

"Oh, no," groaned Rachel under her breath.

"Who's there?" cried out Chip Hoover—half angry, half afraid.

Andy ducked under a bush, but the Mudsharks had already spotted him.

"All right," called out Sarah. "Come on out! We saw you!"

Andy stood up sheepishly.

"Andy West!" cried Billy. "What are you doing here?"

"I'd say it's pretty clear what he's doing here," said Chip. "He's spying on us!"

"You guys are something!" cried Rachel, coming out of her hiding place. "You steal our mascot and then you accuse *us* of spying on you!"

"Steal *your* mascot?" repeated Sarah. "What are you talking about?"

By now, Seth and Zach were also on their feet.

"We'll show you what we're talking about!" yelled Zach. He rushed back into the clearing through the opening. The others quickly followed him.

The dog was lying down in the shadows, gnawing contently on a marrowbone.

"Come here, H.P.!" called Zach. "How are you, boy?"

The dog's ears perked up and it rose to face Zach. It

51

was a small boxer with a tan coat and white markings. It looked suspiciously at Zach and began to growl.

Zach was flabbergasted. "This isn't H.P." he said.

"Of course it isn't," said Chip Hoover. "This is Bowser, the new Mudshark mascot. Now will you tell us what you guys are doing here?"

7 A Mysterious Message

Rachel looked down at the unfriendly boxer in utter amazement. "This is your new mascot?" she asked.

"That's right," replied Billy Butler. "And you guys better not say a word about him to anyone else. We brought him here to keep him a secret until our game against you on Tuesday."

"I don't believe it!" exclaimed Seth. "And all along we thought you were holding H.P. here!"

Sarah Fine looked puzzled. "H.P.?" she said. "What would we be doing with *your* mascot?"

"H.P.'s missing," explained Zach. "We can't find him anywhere. When we saw Billy riding along with those marrowbones we got suspicious. We followed him here."

"You mean you thought we stole your dog?" said

Chip, who gave the Sluggers an angry glare. "That's really nice of you."

"You can't blame us for being suspicious," spoke up Andy. "I mean, you guys were kind of jealous of us for having a mascot, weren't you?"

"So is every other team in the league," countered Sarah. "Why don't you see if any of them stole your dog?"

Rachel shook her head. "I don't think that's likely," she said. "From what we've heard nearly every team is looking for a mascot of their own. Why would any of them steal ours if they were about to get their own mascot?"

Billy scratched Bowser behind one ear. "Maybe H.P. just ran away," he said. "After all, he ran away from his previous owner, didn't he?"

The Sluggers had to admit that this was a possibility. "If he did run away, we'll find him," replied Rachel. "Anyway, I guess we're sorry we accused you guys."

Sarah and Billy said nothing, but Chip grinned. "It's okay," he said. "After all, we are arch-rivals. And you Sluggers never get things right!"

The Sluggers sensed that Chip and the others felt a little bad about H.P.

"Okay, we'll always be enemies on the field," said Seth. "But just tell us if you see H.P. He might show up in Daisy Park."

"If he does, Bowser will chase him out of here fast enough," said Billy, petting the dog's sleek tan coat.

"H.P. can hold his own with any dog," Zach replied. "All we're worried about is finding him."

"I hope you do find him," said Chip. "So then we can find out on Tuesday who's the better dog and the better team."

"Don't worry, we will," said Rachel. "Come on, guys. Let's go."

"So long, Bowser," said Zach. The boxer showed him a mouthful of teeth. "Don't forget to keep smiling."

"He knows who his friends are," said Billy with a snicker.

"And his relatives too," cracked Zach. "You know, you and Bowser could be cousins, Billy."

Rachel, Andy, and Seth laughed as they headed for their bikes.

"We'll see who's laughing after Tuesday's game!" yelled Billy after them.

On the ride home, the Sluggers reviewed the situation.

"I hate to admit it," said Seth, with a sigh. "But maybe Billy's right. Maybe H.P. just ran away."

"If he did, we'll find him," repeated Andy. "We'll put up signs all over town with Rachel and Zach's phone number and address. We could even put an ad in the Lost and Found column of the *Lotus Times*. Someone is bound to have seen H.P."

"That's a great idea," said Rachel. "But let's not forget that there's at least one other suspect who had a motive for taking our mascot."

"Mr. Leopold," said Zach.

"Exactly," replied Rachel. "He's just mean enough to steal H.P. for chasing his dumb old cat."

"If H.P. bothered his cat again, wouldn't he call the dog warden?" reasoned Andy. "And in that case, the dog warden would have given you a warning before taking H.P. away."

"Maybe the dog warden came by, found nobody home, and took H.P. to the pound just to satisfy your neighbor," said Seth. "We should give the dog pound a call just to make sure."

"Fine. Let's call from the phone booth on the corner," said Zach.

Zach called the dog warden and learned that no dog fitting H.P.'s description had been found.

Andy looked concerned. "You don't think, then, that this Mr. Leopold is mean enough to have taken H.P. himself, do you?"

"I'm not sure," said Rachel. "But I'm going to find out."

As night settled in, the four friends parted and headed for their respective homes. Rachel and Zach hoped to find H.P. barking happily at them on the front lawn after returning from a jaunt around the neighborhood. But there was no dog to greet them.

"Nothing new to report," said Mr. Langlin. "Nobody in the neighborhood has seen the dog. But don't worry! He'll be back. Home Plate has a good home here and he's not going to give it up."

Zach and Rachel explained what had happened at Daisy Park and why they were so late getting home.

"Leave it to the competition to jump on the bandwagon," muttered their father when they had finished.

"By next week, every team in the league will have a mascot. Oh, well, we were still the first."

They all ate their dinner in silence. Even Mrs. Langlin's special Southern fried chicken seemed tasteless. Afterward, the family quietly watched television in the den. About eight-thirty Rachel went outside to check the yard one last time. She called out H.P.'s name, but the only response was the chirping of the crickets.

Rachel went up to her bedroom. As she lay on her bed, she reviewed all the day's events. The last thing on her mind before she fell asleep was H.P.'s happy face.

8 Rachel Strikes Out

Rachel woke up late but well rested on Sunday morning. She bounded out of her bed and went downstairs to the kitchen. No one was there.

Rachel found a note from her parents saying they had taken Zach to get new sneakers and would be back soon. It was then she noticed that the red light on the telephone answering machine was flashing. The new message tape her father had bought the day before was next to the machine and the old tape was still inside. Her father hadn't bothered to put the new one in yet.

Rachel remembered that the machine had been on while the family was out looking for H.P. In all the activity since then, no one had played the message back or had bothered to shut off the machine.

Maybe someone had called about H.P.! Rachel rewound the tape and played back the message.

There was a crackle of noise from the worn tape and

then a voice began to speak. It was impossible to recognize the voice through the tape noise and even harder to understand what it was saying.

Then all of a sudden, Rachel heard four words clearly that made her ears prick up. ". . . I took the dog," said the voice. There was a brief pause and then the voice continued. "If you want to see him again, come by . . ." The rest of the sentence was drowned out by the static on the tape. Then the final beep sounded, indicating the end of the message. It was followed by silence.

"Oh, no!" cried Rachel.

She immediately rewound the tape and played it again. Rachel strained her ears, but still couldn't make out another word of the message. What did become clearer the second time, however, was the quality of the voice itself. It was definitely low-pitched.

Mr. Leopold has a low-pitched voice, Rachel thought at once. *But if he took H.P., why would he admit to it on the phone?*

Rachel had no answer. It was possible the dog had got loose while they were out and chased Mr. Leopold's cat, Maisy, again. Perhaps Mr. Leopold caught H.P. in the act and locked him in his house. He had no intention of keeping or harming the dog but just wanted to teach Zach and Rachel a lesson. That would explain the message on the machine.

Rachel lifted the curtain on the kitchen window and looked across the yard. The Leopolds' car was pulling out of the driveway.

Almost without thinking, Rachel went out the door. She headed across her yard toward the Leopolds' house. Rachel then climbed the small fence that separated her yard from the Leopolds' and cautiously skirted around Mr. Leopold's rose bushes.

Rachel now stood safely out of sight behind the Leopolds' house. She stared into the rear windows of the kitchen and living room. There was no sign of any movement inside.

Rachel then moved over to the small rear door of the garage. Taking a deep breath, she leaned lightly against the door to look through the small windows. To her surprise, the door swung wide open. It made an awful creaking sound. The garage was now half in light and half in shadows.

Suddenly feeling afraid and guilty, Rachel froze in the doorway and peered inside. The center of the garage, where the car normally sat, was empty. But piled up against the wall near the door were boxes and garden equipment.

As Rachel's eyes adjusted to the partial darkness, she could see farther into the corners of the garage. Suddenly she heard a box fall to the floor. Something moved quickly across the garage. It looked like the shadow of an animal scrambling for cover.

"H.P.?" Rachel called hopefully, her heart beating fast.

All at once, the entire garage was filled with noise and sunlight. The Leopolds' car was back in the driveway and their automatic door opener was lifting the garage door. The light lit up Mr. Leopold's yellow cat on the garage floor. It stared up at Rachel with glowing eyes.

"Maisy!" Rachel cried.

The cat leaped by her and out the open rear door. Rachel stood frozen with fright as the garage door continued to open. The Leopolds were home! In another moment she would be discovered.

Rachel stepped back and closed the rear door. She considered going back the way she'd come. But Rachel was afraid she'd be caught red-handed either in the Leopolds' yard or climbing over their fence. Instead, she ran around the side of the house and out onto the sidewalk.

Rachel started at a quick walk for her own house. Then a voice called out to her.

"Rachel. Rachel, dear!" called Mrs. Leopold, coming out from the garage.

Rachel stopped dead in her tracks, unable to speak. She was standing directly in front of the Leopolds' house. There was no way she could ignore Mrs. Leopold without drawing even more attention to herself.

"Hi," she replied feebly.

"Why, what's the matter with you?" asked Mrs. Leopold, drawing closer. "You look as if you had just seen a ghost."

"I was just on my way home," replied Rachel, unable to hide either her anxiety or her guilt.

Mr. Leopold was standing by his wife's side. He stared at Rachel with deep concern. "Wait just a minute, Rachel," he said in a firm voice. "I want to talk to you."

Rachel felt a strong impulse to run, but she knew it would only make her look more guilty. She wished that she had never set foot in the Leopolds' yard.

Rachel stood there helplessly as Mr. Leopold approached her. He stopped a few feet from Rachel and looked directly into her eyes.

"I just want you to know how sorry I am," said Mr. Leopold, after a long pause.

"Sorry?" said Rachel in complete surprise. "Sorry for what?"

Mr. Leopold smiled and for the first time Rachel noticed that his face could actually look kindly.

"I saw your father earlier this morning," explained Mr. Leopold. "He told us about your dog running away."

He paused to take in the puzzled look on Rachel's face. "I know," he continued, "you probably thought I'd be glad when I heard the news. Well, I must admit I was pretty mad at your dog when he went after my Maisy. But, aside from that, I like all animals. I know if my Maisy ever ran away from home I'd feel terrible."

Suddenly Rachel remembered the cat running out of the garage. Had she let Maisy run away too? Just then the cat appeared, much to Rachel's relief. She rubbed up against Mr. Leopold's leg and purred loudly.

"Here she is," Mr. Leopold said, picking up the cat. "Now, Maisy, you haven't seen Rachel's doggie, have you?"

Maisy looked at Rachel with accusing eyes that sent a shiver down her back. *It's a lucky thing for me that cats can't talk!* Rachel thought.

"I hope you find your dog soon," said Mrs. Leopold. "You might think about placing an ad in the newspaper. That often works."

"Thank you," said Rachel, finally finding her voice. "That's just what I plan to do."

She exchanged good-byes with the couple and then quickly walked back to her own house.

Rachel immediately went up to her bedroom. How could she have been so wrong about Mr. Leopold? There was no doubt that he was sincerely concerned about H.P.

Obviously, H.P. was not at the Leopolds'. Yet how could she explain the message on the answering machine? If it wasn't Mr. Leopold's voice she had heard, whose was it?

Rachel thought carefully about everything. She couldn't wait for her family to get home so she could tell them about the tape and about the Leopolds. About ten minutes later, the Langlins' car pulled into their driveway. From her bedroom window, Rachel could see Zach bolt from the backseat of the car. He then ran back and forth across their lawn. Zach always made a big deal of breaking in new sneakers.

When Zach finally seemed to be running out of steam, Rachel called to him and her parents.

"Meet me in the kitchen," she yelled. "I have something important for you to hear."

Rachel raced down the stairs.

"What's up, Rach?" Zach gasped as he entered the kitchen.

"I discovered a valuable piece of evidence this morning," revealed Rachel. "It proves that H.P. *was* kidnapped."

"What?" Zach said loudly, getting back his breath. "You mean it *was* Mr. Leopold?"

"No," replied his sister. "He's been removed from the suspect list."

"What's this about Mr. Leopold? asked Mr. Langlin.

"I'll explain it all later," said Rachel. But right now, I want all of you to listen to something incredible."

Before anyone could say another word, Rachel flicked on the answering machine and pressed Playback. The tape played the same broken message Rachel heard before:

". . . I took the dog . . . If you want to see him again, come by . . ."

The family listened in silence as the mysterious voice was lost in static noise.

"It's the dognapper!" cried Zach. "He left a message and instructions for us to follow but we can't hear what they are!"

"Now let's not jump to conclusions," said Mr. Langlin. "You kids have a way of turning everything into a deep, dark mystery. There may be a completely logical explanation for this message."

"All right, Dad," said Rachel. "If there's a logical explanation, let's hear it."

"Well," said Mr. Langlin, thinking a moment,

"maybe it was Aunt Pearl who called. Maybe she took H.P. home to fit him for that mascot sweater I talked to her about for our next game."

"That's not Pearl's voice," said Mrs. Langlin. "It's too low! It sounds like a man. Anyhow, Aunt Pearl would never take H.P. home without asking us first."

"The way that tape's all garbled, I don't think we can be sure if it's a man or woman talking," said Zach. Rachel had to agree with him.

"There's only one way to find out if it was Aunt Pearl," Rachel reasoned, "and that's to call her right now."

Mrs. Langlin did just that and found Aunt Pearl was as surprised to hear about H.P.'s disappearance as everyone else.

"Does anybody else have any more theories about whose voice is on the tape?" Rachel asked.

"Well, it certainly wasn't the dog warden," said Zach. "I phoned the pound last night on the way home from Daisy Park. And they didn't have H.P."

"There is one more call we should make," said Mrs. Langlin. "The police."

She phoned the police station and gave them all the information about H.P. and his disappearance. The police said they'd be on the lookout for the dog, but couldn't promise anything.

"Let's face it," said Rachel. "Whoever left that message has H.P. and the chances are they're not going to give him back without our following their instructions—instructions we don't have because the message is garbled."

"If only I'd changed that message tape yesterday!" said Mr. Langlin.

"Fixing blame won't help," said Mrs. Langlin. "Now all we can do is hope that whoever called, calls again."

Rachel had a sinking feeling in her stomach that it just wouldn't happen.

9 Finally Getting the Message

"You want to steal a base," said Coach Terwilliger. "What's the most important thing to remember?"

"To run fast," replied Rachel.

"Wrong!" replied the coach.

Rachel frowned. It was Monday afternoon and she wanted to be out looking for H.P., not sitting on a bench in Bloom Field being quizzed by her coach during a special practice. Zach, Andy, Seth, and Michelle didn't look any more eager to be putting in extra time. Especially since the added practice was primarily for Rachel's benefit and not theirs.

"Come on, Rachel," said the coach. "Stop daydreaming and think. What's the most important part of stealing a base?"

Rachel tried. "Knowing when the time is right to steal?" she said uncertainly.

"And how do you know that?" the coach asked.

"By watching the pitcher?" Andy offered.

"Not just the pitcher," replied the coach, "but watching everyone else on the field—from the infielders, to the base coaches, to your own batter. But the pitcher is the most important one to keep your eye on. After all, the pitcher's got the ball!"

"That's me!" cried Zach, taking a comic bow.

"Save the humor for the folks in the stands," said the coach dryly. "Okay, Zach is on the mound and, Rachel, you're on third base. There's one out and Seth's up. You know it's now or never for stealing home. Who do you look at?"

"The pitcher," said Rachel with a bit more confidence in her voice.

"Good," said the coach. "But you've got to do more than *look* at him. You've got to closely observe his every movement so you can predict what he's going to do next."

Rachel looked befuddled. "How can I do that?" she asked.

"Read his mind," said Michelle.

"In Zach's case that shouldn't be very hard," said Rachel. "There's never more than a sentence in there at any time!"

Coach Terwilliger ignored the crack. "Maybe Rachel can't read Zach's mind. But she can tell what he's thinking by watching his movements. Zach, get out on the mound and throw a pitch to Andy at home. Rachel, you get on third and keep your eyes open."

Zach trotted out onto the field and hurled a fastball at the catcher.

"Did you see what he did before he threw the ball?" the coach asked Rachel.

"Yes," she replied. "He turned his head from looking at me on third and dropped his chin."

"No, I didn't," protested Zach. "Did I?"

Coach Terwilliger grinned broadly. "You did, champ," he said. "It was a reflex that you probably didn't even think about doing. Which is why you aren't sure you did it. Most pitchers do the same thing. They move in the direction they're going to throw the ball, before they make the pitch."

Rachel was beginning to catch on. "So I should look for that movement before I try to steal a base. Then I'll be able to decide whether the pitcher is going to throw the ball over the plate or throw it *way* wide for a pitchout."

"Exactly," beamed the coach. "And don't forget you need a play on the ball *before* your attempt to steal home. So watch the pitcher's delivery and check to see how prepared your batter is to swing. You also have to see if the infielders are playing short enough to make that fast throw home. And don't forget to look for my steal sign."

"So I've got to watch everything," laughed Rachel. "I mean, I have to be aware of all the signs that point to a good—or bad—time to steal home. And I have to watch for you running your hand down your arm—the old steal sign."

The coach smiled. "You've got it," he said. "It's not easy, but it can be done. If you can read the signs properly, it can give you that little edge. It can be the difference between making it home or being tagged out reaching for the plate."

"I think I'm ready to try it, Coach," said Rachel, after thinking everything over.

"Okay," said the coach. "Seth's at bat, Michelle's playing third, and Andy's behind the plate. It's the bottom of the last inning. There's one out and Rachel's itching to make it in from third. Action!"

Seth stepped up to the plate and took some practice swings. Zach stared at Rachel and then looked for Andy's sign. Andy relayed a special signal from the coach. Zach nodded his head in agreement.

Rachel leaned forward and watched Zach go into his windup. She saw Seth ready himself for a powerful swing. All signals were "go," she decided. As the ball approached the plate, Rachel sprang forward.

But, at the last moment, Andy jumped two feet up the third-base line. It was a well-disguised pitchout! Seth missed the ball by at least a foot. Andy just grabbed the wide pitch and waited for Rachel to run into the tag. She never had a chance.

"Rats!" Rachel cried.

"Halfway there," laughed the coach. "You watched, but you didn't wait! You have to look at one or two pitches to see how everyone's reacting to them. It gives you more of a chance to read telltale signs. And you also should look for my steal signal. Then you make your move."

The coach then changed his approach. He took out a stopwatch and had Rachel run the bases. First she ran them one at a time, and then all the way around to home. They drilled for twenty minutes, until Rachel's legs felt like rubber bands. But having the coach call out advice and encouragement helped. It gave Rachel key points to focus on.

Rachel improved her speed and anticipation each time she ran. She made every movement count. Finally, when the coach had her try to steal home again, she made it easily. Rachel slid in well ahead of the ball.

"That's enough for today," said the coach. "Rachel, you're starting to look like a pro out there. With any luck, your base stealing will help us gain a run or two tomorrow against those Mudsharks."

"I'll try my best," said the right fielder. "Thanks for taking the time to help me, Coach."

Then Rachel turned to her teammates. "You guys too," she added.

"I didn't mind helping you with the practice," said Zach. "But I must admit I felt funny not being out there looking for H.P."

"I just hope we can win tomorrow without H.P. there to cheer—I mean *bark*—us on to victory," said Andy.

"We'll all miss him," said the coach. "That dog really gave us a lift. He loves baseball, all right!"

Rachel thought about telling the coach about the message on the machine but decided not to for the moment. He had enough on his mind with the game tomorrow and didn't need to be worrying about a mysterious voice.

She and Zach did share this new development with

their two best friends, however, after Michelle left. Together they walked their bikes out toward the entrance to the park.

"Some luck!" exclaimed Seth. "A garbled message from a dognapper! If he doesn't hear from you, we may never see H.P. again!"

"Maybe he'll call back," said Andy more hopefully. "Even a dognapper might want to give the message more than once—to make sure you get it straight."

"In the meantime we've got a game against the Mud-sharks tomorrow," sighed Zach. "And with their new mascot, they're going to have the winning edge."

"Maybe we should start thinking about getting another mascot," Seth said.

Zach, Rachel, and Andy just stared at him.

"Hey, no offense," Seth said quickly. "But like Zach says, we can't face the Mudsharks without a mascot—even if it's just a temporary replacement."

Seth was making sense. But Rachel wasn't ready to give up hope of finding H.P.

"I know how important it is for our team to have a mascot when we go up against the Mudsharks," said Rachel. "And we all want that mascot to be H.P. But right now I'm more concerned about finding out that H.P. is okay."

"So am I," added Zach. "I'm really worried about that dog."

Mr. Leopold was no longer a suspect and neither were the Mudsharks. But *someone* had taken the dog and then called to tell them about it. If only they knew who that person was.

The Sluggers continued to discuss the mystery as they rode their bikes. Soon they were at Zach and Rachel's house. The four friends went into the Langlins' yard.

"We've still got some unanswered questions," Andy said.

"Like what?" asked Seth.

"Like where is H.P.?" said Rachel. "And who took him?"

"And how can we find that person?" added Zach.

"Well, we've already eliminated Mr. Leopold and the Mudsharks," said Seth. "That takes care of the only likely suspects *we* know."

"What about suspects we *don't* know?" piped in Andy. "Like a real dognapper—a stranger?"

"Maybe it was neither a real dognapper *nor* somebody we know," said Rachel.

Zach, Andy, and Seth all turned to Rachel with a puzzled look. They didn't have a clue to what she was talking about.

"Maybe H.P.'s owner took him," said Rachel.

"That's right," said Zach. "He could have seen our signs and come to get his dog back. After all, the signs had both our address and phone number on them."

"Why are we bothering?" asked Andy sadly. "If it's a real dognapper, then H.P.'s gone. And if his owner took him back, H.P.'s still gone for good."

"Maybe so," said Rachel. "But if his owner took him, I want a chance to say good-bye. I also want to be sure the owner will take good care of him."

"Yeah," said Zach. "And I want to make sure H.P.

has the rubber ball and squeaky toy we bought him!"

"We could ask the owner to let H.P. be our mascot for one more game against the Mudsharks," said Andy. "It would give us a big lift in an important game."

"Well, whether the owner or a dognapper has H.P., we still don't have any clues to finding either of them," sighed Seth.

"Oh yes, we do!" cried Rachel, suddenly excited. "If the owner took H.P., we have one good clue that we've overlooked."

"Like what?" said Seth.

"Like H.P.'s tag," answered Rachel. "Remember the insignia with the two bats and a ball?"

Rachel picked up a long stick and drew two crossed bats in the dirt—with a baseball beneath them.

"It looked like this," she said.

"Of course!" yelled Zach. "And that gives us a second clue. Let's not forget that H.P. loves baseball."

"The way H.P. is drawn to baseball fields," said Andy, "maybe his owner isn't just a fan like we first thought. That insignia could mean he's part of a team."

"Precisely," said Rachel. "He's probably one of the players on a team."

"If we can find out what club the insignia stands for," said Seth, "we should be able to track down H.P.'s owner."

"One thing for sure," said Zach. "That insignia doesn't belong to any local Youth League team or Major League club."

"Then what about a semipro team?" said Andy. "One of the teams that came in to play the Lotus Pines Hawks recently."

"If it's a regional semipro team, their official yearbook should be in the bookstore around the corner," said Seth. "And each team's insignia would be right on the cover."

"What are we waiting for?" said Rachel. "Let's go over there right now!"

The four friends entered the bookstore and went straight to the sports section. They found the shelf with the twenty-odd official yearbooks and started checking covers.

"Here it is!" cried Zach, holding up a yearbook.

There was the insignia. And underneath it were the words "Bakerville Bombers."

"I know the Bombers!" said Andy excitedly. "My folks took me to see them play against the Lotus Pines Hawks last season."

"Well, it looks like they've been in town more recently," said Rachel. "*Somehow* H.P. got away from his owner—one of the Bombers—and ended up on our playing field."

"Bloom Field is only about a mile from the Hawks' stadium," said Zach. "H.P. could have covered that distance easily when he ran away."

Rachel copied down something from the yearbook. Then she walked outside to the phone booth on the corner.

"Who are you calling?" asked Andy.

"The office of the Bakerville Bombers," she said.

Rachel dialed, listened intently for a minute, and then hung up the phone with a frown.

"No answer?" asked Zach.

"No, it was a taped message," said his sister. "It said that the Bombers were on the road and wouldn't be back in town until next week. Then it gave some dates for their home games."

"Look, I know how much we all miss H.P." said Seth. "But we really have to find some sort of mascot for tomorrow's game against the Mudsharks."

"Well," sighed Andy, "if H.P.'s owner took him, it looks like he won't be coming back in any case."

Rachel said nothing. The idea of losing H.P. was much more upsetting to her than any possible defeat at the hands of the Mudsharks.

Tuesday, after school, Rachel arrived home late for the big game. She had gone around to the store owners where she had put up the Lost Dog signs. She hoped one of them might have talked to the man from the Bakerville Bombers and might have more information about him. But her investigation turned up no new leads.

When Rachel finally walked in the door, Zach and her parents were all ready to leave for the game.

"I'm sorry about H.P., honey," said her father, who had heard the latest developments. "Maybe, if it is a member of the Bakerville Bombers, he'll try to contact you again sometime soon. Right now, though, you've got a baseball game to play. Why don't you get into your uniform?"

Rachel turned her attention to the game. Maybe with some luck, and her new confidence as a base stealer, they just might beat the Mudsharks yet. But she also knew that without H.P. to boost up their spirits, the odds were against them.

"Why don't you go ahead?" suggested Rachel. "I'll ride my bike over to the field."

Mr. Langlin considered this briefly. "Well, all right," he said. "But don't be late!"

Rachel assured him she wouldn't be. Then she waved to her family as they pulled out of the driveway.

Rachel went up to her room and flipped on the radio as she changed into her uniform. She heard an announcement for the Lotus Pines Hawks and let out a happy cry. Then she ran downstairs to the phone in the kitchen.

Rachel dialed the Lotus Pines Hawks' office and spoke briefly to a man who answered the phone. She asked him a couple of questions and got the answers she was hoping for. She thanked the man and hung up. Then she quickly put a new announcement on the answering machine for her parents. She knew they would be calling when she didn't show up at the game on time.

When she finished, Rachel rushed out the door and jumped onto her bike. She didn't know if the plan rapidly forming in her mind would work. Still, she had to give it a try. She rode her bike out into the street. But it *wasn't* toward Bloom Field that she now headed.

10 The Return of Home Plate

"We, the Mudsharks, would like to present our new mascot—Bowser, the Battling Boxer!"

Chip Hoover's announcement, just before the start of the game, was greeted with enthusiastic applause by the Mudshark fans. The Southside Sluggers felt flat-out dejected.

Out marched Bowser onto the field. He was followed by a proud Billy Butler, who held his leash. Bowser wore a cape of red and yellow—the Mudsharks' colors—on his back. The cape was tied by a string around his thick neck. The outlandish costume reminded Zach of an animal superhero.

"They make a swell pair," Zach muttered. "Amazing Dog and his pet Boy."

"If H.P. were here he'd show up that strutting boxer," murmured Susan Stein.

Coach Terwilliger had more important things on his mind than the Mudsharks' mascot. "Has Rachel shown up yet?" he asked her brother.

"Nope," said Zach. "I can't understand it. She said she'd be right over."

The coach walked over to the stands. He was beginning to worry about his right fielder. Rachel had never been late for a game before.

"Rachel's not here yet, folks!" Coach Terwilliger yelled up into the stands.

Mr. and Mrs. Langlin shook their heads in response. They were worried too.

"I'm going to call home and see if she's still there," said Mr. Langlin.

Mrs. Langlin nodded and her husband quickly headed for the pay phone in the parking lot.

Coach Terwilliger couldn't delay the start of the game any longer. He was forced to put Artie Wilson, a skinny kid with wavy brown hair, in right field.

Seth groaned when he saw Artie amble out toward the outfield. Although he wasn't a bad hitter, Artie had an almost uncontrollable fear of flying balls headed in his direction. Seth was prepared to go back to being "Clear Out" Bradigan. He was ready to cover right and left field until Rachel arrived.

The Mudsharks' first batter, Lisa Choi, stepped up to the plate. Robin Hayes, put in to pitch the first two innings, easily struck her out with two speedy fastballs and an off-speed pitch.

The next hitter was Sarah Fine. She outran a slow

grounder to third for a base hit. Then, Chip Hoover, usually a strong hitter, popped out with a high foul that Andy snagged with no trouble. Maybe Chip had been taking care of Bowser when he should have been practicing his batting.

Big Joe Jones, however, needed no practice. He sent Robin's first pitch way over Artie's head in right field. Artie watched the ball bounce against the fence before he reacted. By the time Seth ran over and tracked the ball down, Sarah was crossing home plate and Joe was approaching third.

Then Big Joe went too far. Slow as he was, Joe decided to pass up a sure triple and try for a homer. As Joe rounded third, Seth launched a perfect relay throw to Luis at second. Luis then pegged the ball into Andy in front of home plate. Big Joe was caught in a rundown between Andy and Michelle. After a couple of quick throws, and making Joe run back and forth a few times, Michelle finally tagged him out trying to dive back into third.

As the Sluggers trotted in, Seth smiled at Andy.

"Who does Big Joe think he is?" asked Seth. "He certainly doesn't run those bases like Rachel. Maybe we should invite Big Joe to our next special baserunning practice."

Meanwhile, Mr. Langlin returned to his seat in the stands.

"Was Rachel home?" asked his wife anxiously.

"No, but she left a message for us on the answering machine," said Mr. Langlin, "and everything's okay."

Mrs. Langlin looked confused. "What do you mean it's okay? Where is Rachel?"

Mr. Langlin smiled and told her what the message said.

"This is great," Mrs. Langlin said. "I just hope Rachel's hunch is right."

"So do I," said her husband.

Then they turned their attention back to the game.

The Sluggers didn't score any runs in the bottom of the first inning. Artie looked nervous batting lead-off and grounded out. Susan didn't do any better. And Seth flied deep to center for his out.

The Mudsharks, however, scored again when Phil Woods smashed the ball hard to right field. Poor Artie Wilson took one look up at the ball whizzing toward him and jumped out of the way. Susan rushed over from center field and tried to run the ball down. But it was too late. Phil was speeding around third and heading home before the ball had even reached the infield. He crossed home plate at a trot, to make the score 2–0.

"Rachel would have made that catch easily," said Seth, who felt a little guilty about not trying for the ball himself. "I sure hope she gets here soon."

"It's not like Rachel to miss a game," said Susan. "First H.P. disappears and now her. What next?"

"I wouldn't mind seeing Artie Wilson disappear," joked Seth. "I think the two of us can cover this outfield better without him."

From this point on, the Sluggers' morale on the field went from bad to worse. The Mudsharks' new mascot didn't help matters, either. From his honored seat in the stands, Bowser barked every time the Mudsharks got a hit. It wasn't a happy bark like H.P.'s. But the noise he generated seemed to be picked up by the Mudsharks fans. And there was something very depressing about a bunch of excited fans barking for your opponents.

The bottom of the second inning was a disaster for the Sluggers. Marty dropped a bunt in front of the plate—and was tagged out from *behind* by the Mudsharks' catcher, Chip Hoover. Andy, known as the "Windmill" for his wild swings, lived up to his nickname. He whooshed up three straight strikes. Luis walked to first when Ken Allan started losing a little control. Michelle stopped Luis in his tracks with a hot grounder that ricocheted off his foot halfway to second. Luis was called out for interfering with the play.

The third inning was about to begin, with the Mudsharks leading by two runs. Mr. Langlin glanced off beyond the playing field and excitedly nudged his wife.

"What is it?" Mrs. Langlin asked.

"Look out there," he said, pointing to a lone figure on a bicycle approaching the field.

Mrs. Langlin stood up and cupped one hand over her eyes to block out the sun. "It's Rachel!" she exclaimed. "And look what she's got in her bike basket!"

Coach Terwilliger, down on the field, had spotted Rachel too. "I'll be doggoned!" he muttered. "She's got our pooch with her!"

It was true. In Rachel's basket sat Home Plate himself. The shaggy little dog looked happier than ever to be back in the ballpark. Behind them was a man in a red sportscar. He parked just off the field and hopped out of his car. He wore a baseball uniform.

But everyone's eyes were fixed on Rachel and the dog. As Rachel stopped her bike near the stands, H.P. leaped out of the basket. He ran playfully around the field, acknowledging the cheers and applause of the Sluggers fans. The only one in the stands who seemed upset by H.P.'s sudden appearance was Bowser. The "Battling Boxer" jumped down from his seat and growled at the intruder.

H.P. turned to face the other dog. He stretched out his short legs and stood his ground. He growled back at the boxer. Bowser moved closer and snarled, baring his teeth.

Zach, Seth, and the other Sluggers were beginning to get nervous. Even Rachel was worried. Bowser was nearly twice the size of H.P. and looked ten times as mean.

"Go on, Bowser!" cried Billy Butler. "Show that runt who's top dog on this field!"

"Hey!" shouted Rachel. "I don't want H.P. to get hurt!"

But H.P. looked happily at his friends and kept barking at Bowser. Then he slunk way down close to the ground and gave Bowser a deep, menacing growl. Bowser showed no interest in living up to his "Battling Boxer" nickname. He backed up a step and gave a half-hearted bark back.

Encouraged by this, H.P. advanced on the bigger dog, barking loudly and scratching at the ground. A few feet away from Bowser, H.P. leaped toward the other dog. Bowser whined and jumped away before H.P. could reach him. When H.P. attacked again, the mighty boxer scampered off the field.

Billy Butler's jaw dropped half a foot. "Bowser!" he cried. "Get back here! Where do you think you're going?"

"Probably home to his doghouse!" called out Zach from the sidelines. "You'd better tell him to leave some room for the rest of you Mudsharks! You'll be joining him there soon enough!"

Bowser's unexpected retreat and Zach's wisecrack had the entire crowd laughing heartily.

"That's showing them, pooch!" cried Coach Terwilliger. "Rachel, I don't know where you've been, but I'm glad you're back."

By now the man in the baseball uniform was standing by Rachel's side.

Coach Terwilliger looked at him with surprise. "Say, aren't you Ray Fox, the catcher for the Bakerville Bombers?"

"That's me," smiled Ray.

The other Sluggers had gathered around Ray Fox and Rachel.

"How did you find H.P., Sis?" Zach asked Rachel. "Where did you find the Bombers?"

"I'll explain it all later," Rachel replied. "But right now we've got a ball game to win."

"I couldn't agree more," said the coach. "Everybody get to your positions. Zach, get out there on the mound. And Rachel, get out to right field where you belong."

Artie looked depressed. "Does this mean I've been replaced?" he asked the coach.

"I'm afraid so, Artie," said the coach. "But I have another job for you and it's an important one. I want you to keep an eye on H.P. Make sure he doesn't take off after that big, bully boxer. We need him here."

Artie brightened. The idea of watching the game with the shaggy puppy appealed to him a lot more than dodging fly balls in the outfield.

"Ray, Why don't you stay and watch the rest of the game?" asked Coach Terwilliger.

"I wouldn't miss it for the world," said Ray Fox with a grin.

11 Taking Home Plate

Home Plate's remarkable return raised the Sluggers' spirits. But the Mudsharks didn't just give up. The confrontation between the two dogs made them more angry than discouraged. The Mudsharks played harder than ever.

Thanks to Zach's pitching, though—and good fielding by Rachel, Seth, and Susan—the Mudsharks were held scoreless in the top of the third.

Ernie led off for the Sluggers in the bottom half of the inning. He smacked the ball straight back to the pitcher, who made a great grab. Zach also got a good piece of a Ken Allan fastball. But his line drive was speared by Big Joe Jones on third. Joe held the ball over his head for several seconds as the Mudsharks yelled and whistled.

Rachel came up to bat with two outs and nobody on base. The Sluggers were starting to slump again in their seats. And she desperately wanted to lift them up.

Rachel's first thought was to go for the *big* extra-base hit. But she knew that one big hit was not the answer. Her real job was to get a two-out rally going. The Sluggers had to put a bunch of hits together.

After patiently taking two close strikes, Rachel decided to call on her speed. She gently tapped a grounder toward Joe Jones at third. Joe lumbered in to pick up the ball early. But by the time he got to it, Rachel was only a few steps away from first base. She beat the throw easily.

Susan Stein then showed some patience of her own. She fouled off three straight fastballs and managed to work the Mudshark pitcher for a rally-saving walk. Now there were runners on first and second with two outs.

Seth stepped into the batter's box next. He leaned over the plate, holding his bat, Thunderbolt, high over his right shoulder. After Seth took one strike and fouled another pitch off, Thunderbolt connected. The ball soared high over second base and carried out beyond Lisa Choi in center field. H.P. barked madly and Slugger fans clapped along.

Rachel sped home with Susan right behind her. Seth held up at third with the score now tied at 2–2. Unfortunately, Marty left Seth stranded on third with a soft fly ball to the Mudshark's shortstop. The rally was over.

In the fourth inning, both teams seemed a bit flat again. Nobody could get on the base paths. And no runs were scored by either club.

The fifth inning got off to a much better start for the Mudsharks. Chip Hoover hit a ground-ball single right over second base. Then Joe Jones made up for botching Rachel's grounder by clubbing a homer over the left-field fence. The Mudsharks jumped to a 4–2 lead.

In the Sluggers' half of the fifth inning, Ernie Peters immediately popped up to Sarah Fine at second base. But Zach, batting ninth, gave the top of the Sluggers' order something to work with. He hit a clean single to right field.

Rachel then delivered with a low line drive to center that put her on first and moved Zach to third. But, anxious to prove her new base-stealing skills, Rachel took off for second base on the first pitch to Susan Stein. She didn't even wait for a steal sign from the coach. It didn't come close to working! Chip Hoover leaped to his feet, grabbed the ball cleanly as it crossed the plate, and easily gunned Rachel down at second.

So, thanks to Rachel's impatience, Susan was now batting with Zach on third and two outs. Susan was suddenly more worried about just keeping the inning alive than scoring a lot of runs.

As it turned out, the Mudsharks' starting pitcher was showing signs of late-in-the-game fatigue. Susan's bunt halfway to first base caught Ken Allan flat-footed. All he could do was hold Zach to third base and let Susan run safely to first.

Seth was then walked intentionally by Ken to load the bases. Ken obviously felt a lot better about pitching to Marty Franklin than to a dangerous hitter like Seth.

Ken soon learned that Marty didn't have to be a dangerous hitter—or any other kind of hitter. He just had to stand there like a statue. Ken's control was melting away down the stretch under the hot sun.

Ken walked Marty on four straight balls. This sent Zach skipping and singing across home plate. With the bases still loaded, the Sluggers now trailed by just one run.

The Mudsharks' coach decided it was time to bring in relief pitcher Rick Waters. It turned out to be a good idea. He struck out Andy with three fastballs to end the rally. The Sluggers were going into the last inning, down 4–3.

Zach pitched fairly well in the top of the sixth inning. But Billy Butler, of all people, still angry about Bowser's defeat, hit a high ball to center field. Susan lost it in the sun and let the ball drop behind her. Billy made it all the way to second.

Lisa Choi then brought Billy home on a shallow shot to right and an error by Rachel. The overly eager right fielder had tried to pick the ball up on one hop and throw out Lisa at first. The rushed throw hooked off toward the stands.

The Mudsharks lead now swelled to 5–3. Rachel seemed to be trying too hard. She was hurting the Sluggers even more than she was helping them.

After Zach chalked up a final strikeout, the Sluggers

came up for their last at bats. Luis promptly wasted an out by lofting the first pitch to shortstop Mike Moran. But Michelle doubled crisply to left and Ernie drove her home with another double down the first-base line.

The Sluggers were alive! With a runner on second and one out, they were only down by a single run. Every player on the bench was up and screaming. Fans were clapping loudly. And H.P. was barking away at Artie's side.

Zach now had a great chance to help save the game. Like most lefties, Zach naturally hit better against right-handed pitchers. He could see the ball coming at him all the way. What's more, Rick Waters's sweeping motion made it particularly easy for lefties to track his pitches.

After two high fastballs, Rick threw a sweeping change-up. Zach zeroed in on the pitch from the moment it left Rick's hand. He bashed the ball to deep right field and cruised to second base. Ernie had no trouble coming around with the tying run.

The tide had shifted for sure. Three doubles in a row had brought the Sluggers even with the Mudsharks. All the Sluggers now felt loose and were yelling for a victory.

The only tense Slugger was Rachel. She was up at bat and desperately wanted to do something right. She needed to bring in the winning run for the team—one way or another.

Zach, perched on second base, was also anxious to score the winning run. When Rachel pushed a fly to short center field, Zach took off. But he had to stop still halfway between second and third to see if the ball was caught. If a Mudshark grabbed it on a fly, Zach had to rush back to second to avoid a double play. If the ball dropped in safely, he could take off for third.

Mike Moran backed up quickly from his shortstop position. Lisa Choi charged straight in from center field. Both watched the ball fall to the grass within inches of their outstretched gloves.

Lisa picked up the ball and noticed that Zach was still frozen between bases. She faked a throw to first. For a split second, Zach believed Lisa was going after Rachel. So, when Lisa swiveled and zipped the ball to Big Joe at third, she was able to nail Zach before he could even begin his slide.

The throw to third allowed the speedy Rachel to make it to second base. With two outs, she was now the Sluggers' lone base runner. And the Sluggers were still a run away from beating the Mudsharks.

The first two pitches to Susan Stein were wicked fastballs. One Susan missed by a mile. The other just missed the strike zone for a ball. Rick seemed to suddenly find his best stuff. In fact, he had the right-handed batter completely off balance.

Rachel was getting nervous—and so was Coach Terwilliger. He gave Rachel the signal to steal. She was shocked!

As the next pitch crossed home plate, Rachel danced off second and just kept going. The Mudsharks were caught totally by surprise. Chip threw off his catcher's mask, but didn't even try to make the throw. Rachel stood safely on third base.

Now the coach called time-out. He motioned both Susan and Rachel to the sidelines.

"Rachel's going to steal home plate!" he announced with a smile. "And I don't mean our mascot."

"But, Coach," said Rachel. "They'll be expecting it."

"Don't disappoint them," he answered. "Just remember what we worked on and keep your eyes open. And Susan—you try to hit the next good pitch on the ground."

Rich watched Rachel intently out of the corner of one eye. Rachel stretched her body toward home plate but kept her back foot anchored firmly on third base. It was just threatening enough to make the pitcher edgy. He waited a long time before going into his windup.

When Rick lowered his chin and brought the ball straight in toward the plate, Rachel glimpsed Susan setting herself for the pitch. Rachel knew this was it! The instant Susan made contact, Rachel's legs started pumping.

Big Joe picked up Susan's grounder to third and decided to try for the shorter throw to home plate. Rachel instinctively threw out both of her legs and went into her slide. In the middle of a cloud of dust, Chip snagged the ball and dove for Rachel's outstretched leg.

"Safe!" cried the umpire, as the dust cleared.

Rachel leaped to her feet. "We win!" she screamed. "We beat the Mudsharks 6–5!"

H.P. led the Sluggers as they charged out to Rachel. The excited dog leaped into Rachel's arms and licked her face. Then everybody was hugging her and cheering.

12 Sparky or H.P.?

As the celebration at home plate began to die down, Rachel could see her mother and father approaching. By their side walked Ray Fox. When they reached Rachel, Ray smiled and tipped his baseball cap.

"Great base running out there," Ray said to Rachel.

Before Rachel could answer, H.P. dashed right past her and jumped into Ray's arms.

"Sparky!" yelled Ray, hugging the dog to him. "You did all right too, boy!"

Zach, Andy, and Seth looked at each other.

"His name is not Sparky!" Zach spoke up. "It's H.P.!"

"No, it's really Ray's dog Sparky," said Rachel quietly. "Before I left the house today to come to the game, I heard an announcement on the radio. It said the Bakerville Bombers—who beat the Hawks Saturday night—were playing the Lotus Pine Hawks again tonight."

"But how did you find Ray so quickly?" asked Andy.

"I called the stadium and the man who answered said the Bombers were on the field practicing for the game. I asked him if one of the Bombers had a dog. The man said there was a shaggy little dog running around the bases. But he wasn't sure who it belonged to."

"So, obviously that shaggy dog was H.P.—I mean, Sparky," said Andy.

"I never did ask you about the name H.P.," said Ray Fox to Rachel. "Why do you call Sparky H.P.? What does it mean?"

"It's short for Home Plate," said Rachel. "We call him that because he kept resting on home plate the day we found him."

Ray laughed. "He used to do the same thing at our field," he said. "I'm glad to see he hasn't changed."

The dog was now resting on home plate with his tail wagging away.

"Anyway, when Rachel showed up, Sparky went right to her arms," continued Ray Fox. "I knew right away that she was the girl who had taken such good care of my dog when he ran away. Rachel told me all about how you made Sparky your team mascot and how you needed him in your big game against the Mudsharks. So I let her bring the little fellow back and followed in my car."

"How did H.P. run away in the first place?" Mrs. Langlin wanted to know.

"I had Sparky for only a month when our team came to Lotus Pines to play the Hawks," said Ray Fox. "I left Sparky with a friend during the game. I came back to get him and my friend said the dog had run away."

"Just like that?" asked Zach.

"Well, he had been playing in the front yard," explained Ray. "And when the letter carrier opened the gate, Sparky just took right off. I tried to find him, but our team had to leave that night to play a game in another town. I didn't get back to Lotus Pines until last Saturday. That's when I saw your Lost Dog sign in a store window."

"That's when you took H.P. from our backyard?" asked Mr. Langlin.

"I came right over to your house and rang the bell," replied Ray. "Nobody answered and then I heard a dog barking in the backyard. I saw it was Sparky. I was so happy to find him—and I figured your signs meant you wanted his owner to claim him."

"But why didn't you leave us a note?" asked Zach.

"I didn't have a pencil or paper. But I called and left a message on your answering machine as soon as I got back to my room," said Ray. "From what Rachel told me, it came out pretty garbled. But how would I know that?"

"What *exactly* did you say in that message anyway?" asked Rachel.

"I said something like 'I'm Ray Fox, the dog's

owner, and *I took the dog* back to my hotel. *If you want to see him again, come by* Hawk Stadium tonight—I left tickets for you.' And when you didn't come to see him, I figured you were glad his owner had finally claimed him."

"Well, no matter what the message said, I guess this is the last time H.P. will be resting on *our* home plate," said Zach sadly.

"He sure was a great mascot," sighed Seth. "I know I'm going to miss him terribly."

Rachel didn't say anything. She just hugged H.P. tightly with tears in her eyes.

Ray Fox watched Rachel and the dog and rubbed his chin. Just then Coach Terwilliger came strolling over the join the group.

"That was a great game, you guys!" exclaimed the coach. "And thanks, Ray, for bringing our mascot back one last time."

"Well, maybe not for the last time," said Ray with a smile.

"What do you mean?" asked Rachel.

Ray looked slightly embarrassed. "Well, I've been offered a place on a Major League team," he said. "I won't mention the team's name because they haven't made their own official announcement yet."

"That's great news," said Zach. "But what does it have to do with H.P.?"

"Quite a lot," said Ray. "My life is going to change when I'm in the majors. I'll be traveling all over the country and I can't take Sparky with me. He'll be on his own almost all the time. I hate to say it—but I'm going to have to find Sparky a new home."

Rachel looked up anxiously at Ray. "If that's true," she asked. "Why didn't you just leave H.P. with us?"

"I didn't know anything about you guys until today," said Ray. "The poster just said to come for the dog. I didn't even know if you wanted to keep Sparky."

"Well, we do!" said Mr. Langlin loudly.

Everybody stared at Mr. Langlin in surprise.

"That's great," smiled Ray. "H.P. needs a good home like yours. And, just as important, he needs to be part of a baseball team."

"That's the first time you called him H.P.!" said Rachel.

"That's because that's his name now," said Ray.

"All *right*!" screamed Rachel. "Thanks so much, Ray. We can't thank you enough!"

Zach, Andy, and Seth started to jump and shout. They took turns hugging and petting H.P. Mr. and Mrs. Langlin also got in a couple of hugs and seemed very happy.

Ray Fox then bent down and gave the shaggy little dog a long, tender embrace. He said he would try to come by to visit from time to time when he could.

Mr. Langlin invited Ray to join their celebration party at the Southside Ice Cream Shop. But Ray said he had to get back to the stadium for his game against the Hawks. Then he said his good-byes and started to walk away.

Home Plate barked and began to run after Ray.

But Ray kept walking and didn't turn around. Suddenly, H.P. stopped and looked at Rachel. Then he barked and ran right back to her.

"Good boy!" cried Rachel, rubbing H.P.'s shaggy head. "Good dog!"

The Southside Ice Cream Shop was filled to capacity with Sluggers, parents, friends, relatives, and one dog. Mr. Langlin, who had a strict rule about no pets inside his shop, made an exception for H.P.

At the table of honor sat Coach Terwilliger, Rachel, Zach, Andy, Seth, Mrs. Langlin, and Aunt Pearl. H.P. was on the floor, dressed in the orange-and-green sweater Aunt Pearl had made for him.

"It's a perfect fit," said Mrs. Langlin to her sister. "You did a great job."

"Well, now he really looks like an official mascot, with the Southside Sluggers' colors on him," said Aunt Pearl proudly.

"Yeah, it's great to have him back," said Coach Terwilliger, who was deep into a dish of vanilla ice cream. "And it's great to have a right fielder who can steal home."

Rachel looked up from her Boysenberry Bash Sundae. "Thanks, Coach," she said. "I'm really sorry about missing a chunk of the game. But I knew H.P. was the only one who could provide that big boost we needed to win."

"Okay," smiled the coach. "We'll let it go this time. But the next time you're late, it's the doghouse for you!"

"Ruff!" barked H.P. from under the table.

"I think H.P.'s reminding us that he's the only one who hasn't been fed yet," said Zach.

"Your father is supposed to be taking care of that," said Mrs. Langlin, looking toward the ice-cream counter. "Where is he?"

Just then the kitchen door swung open and Mr. Langlin emerged carrying a silver bowl full of H.P.'s favorite dog biscuits. The biscuits were topped by a small mountain of ice cream, whipped cream, and a cherry.

"Here it is!" he cried. "The Home Plate Special! I call it a Shaggy Dog Sundae!"

Everyone laughed and Mr. Langlin put the bowl down on the floor. H.P. dug into it with gusto.

"It looks like he loves that sundae as much as he does baseball!" exclaimed Seth.

"Ruff!" barked H.P., showing off his whipped-cream-covered whiskers.

Coach Terwilliger's Corner

Hi there, all you Sluggers!

Stealing home is an honored tradition in professional baseball. Here are some facts about the three top home-plate stealers of all time:

Ty Cobb

Cobb was one of the greatest all-around players in baseball history. He was an outfielder for the Detroit Tigers for most of his professional career. Cobb stole home *thirty-five* times in regular-season play and once in a World Series.

In 1915, he set a long-time American League record of *ninety-six* stolen bases. On June 18 of that year, he stole home *twice* in one game. In three separate games between 1909 and 1912, Cobb stole second, third, and home all in the same inning!

It's no wonder one of his nicknames was the Georgia Tornado. Cobb claimed, however, that his skill at stealing bases was not just a matter of speed. He thought his base stealing relied more on quick wits and aggressiveness.

George J. Burns

Burns was a National League outfielder and first baseman from 1911 to 1925. Burns stole home an amazing *twenty-seven* times.

Frank "Wildfire" Schulte

Schulte had a professional career that stretched from 1904 to 1918. Most of this time he played outfield for the Chicago Cubs. He won the National League's first Most Valuable Player Award in 1911.

Baseball historian Bill James has called Schulte the "best outfield arm" of the first decade of the 1900s. Schulte also had a fabulous pair of legs. He stole home *twenty-two* times.

That's all for now. See you in the next Southside Sluggers Baseball Mystery. Until then, play ball!

Coach Terwilliger